Praises for *Grandma and Me*

"*Grandma and Me* is an amazing gift to parents and grandchildren of those dealing with Alzheimer's. My father has been dealing with Alzheimer's for about 5 years now. Our family, including four grandchildren, often struggle with ways to help my father and each other through this journey. We try to focus on love and solutions. *Grandma and Me* is full of tangible ways young children can help their grandparents and keep that special connection. Thank you to Beatrice, MaryAnn and Julia for putting the words and images together so my children, and so many others, can understand and help love their grandparents through this journey."

Kristen Schottenheimer, Coach, Trainer, Speaker, daughter of
former NFL Coach, Marty Schottenheimer

"I love this! What a beautiful book. It brought tears to my eyes reflecting on how I felt when my grandfather had the disease. This book will help so many families!"

Lisa Merrick, Founder of the Remembering Kay Foundation,
daughter and grand-daughter of loved ones with Alzheimer's disease

"*Grandma and Me* provides real world examples for engaging children with family members who are suffering from dementia. The book will help children understand the illness as well as provide children with ways to continue to help and engage the older family member with compassion and love."

Kelly Morton, PH.D. Professor of Family Medicine,
Professor of Psychology, Loma Linda University

"Wow! Beatrice and Mary Ann take a complicated and difficult journey that is near impossible for even adults to navigate and fully comprehend and embrace the whole family with warmth, comfort and a safe place to explore and process living with a loved one who is transforming through the stages of dementia. *Grandma and Me* helps provide a lighted path for the family as they walk through a forest of emotions together. I love the beautiful images of the grandmother and grandson's relationship as it grows and changes over time. In addition, Beatrice and Mary Ann add a depth of supportive information, insight and suggestions to caregivers of children who may be struggling with the changes within their family."

Emily Nevin, Social Worker and daughter of a
mother who was transformed by dementia

Grandma and Me

Grandma and Me

A Kid's Guide for Alzheimer's and Dementia

Beatrice Tauber Prior, Psy.D.
& Mary Ann Drummond, RN
Illustrator Julia Walther

NEW YORK

LONDON • NASHVILLE • MELBOURNE • VANCOUVER

Grandma and Me

A Kid's Guide for Alzheimer's and Dementia

Published in New York, New York, by Morgan James Publishing. Morgan James is a trademark of Morgan James, LLC. www.MorganJamesPublishing.com

The Morgan James Speakers Group can bring authors to your live event. For more information or to book an event visit The Morgan James Speakers Group at www.TheMorganJamesSpeakersGroup.com.

ISBN 9781683506997 paperback
ISBN 9781683507017 hardcover
ISBN 9781683507000 eBook
Library of Congress Control Number: 2017912052

Cover Design by:
Rachel Lopez
www.r2cdesign.com

Interior Design by:
Chris Treccani
www.3dogcreative.net

In an effort to support local communities, raise awareness and funds, Morgan James Publishing donates a percentage of all book sales for the life of each book to Habitat for Humanity Peninsula and Greater Williamsburg.

Get involved today! Visit www.MorganJamesBuilds.com.

Dedication

Dear Oma—You have the ability to compassionately connect to others no matter where they are on their life's journey. We can share this gift of connection in *Grandma and Me: A Kid's Guide for Alzheimer's and Dementia* because of your example. We are forever grateful.

Dear Family:

If you have picked up this book, you are most likely on a journey with someone who is diagnosed with Alzheimer's disease or a related dementia. You are not alone. Now more than ever families are finding themselves impacted by Alzheimer's disease and other dementias, leaving children to cope with the changed relationships within the family unit. When a loved one is diagnosed with Alzheimer's disease or a related dementia it is often difficult to know how to explain the changes brought on by such a difficult disease. This is especially true when it comes to speaking about the disease with a young child.

This book was written to give adults a gentle, yet age appropriate way to explain what is happening to their loved one who has dementia. By reading the story of *Grandma and Me* with your child, you will ensure their feelings are addressed while providing them with necessary tools to maintain positive interactions for as long as possible with their loved one living with dementia.

Just like adults, children experience a wide array of emotions including sadness, anger, fear, guilt and even a sense of loss when dealing with the serious illness of a close family member. Alzheimer's disease can be especially challenging for a young child as the disease alters how the person they love responds and acts. When children can understand what dementia is, and that the changes in behavior are a result of the disease, they are better able to cope with their feelings. It is important for children to know the changes they see in their loved one's behavior is part of the illness and not directed at, or caused by, the child in any way.

While *Grandma and Me* highlights the journey of Alzheimer's disease, this book is appropriate to share with a young child who's loved one is diagnosed with other forms of dementia. Told from a child's perspective, the story will teach your child how to maintain a relationship with their loved one while finding their special place as part of the family care team.

Beatrice and Mary Ann

My Grandma is the best Grandma ever! She is the kind of Grandma that laughs a lot. She knows everything about everything! She always has candy in her pocket just for me. My favorite candy is butterscotch, the kind with the yellow, crinkly paper. When Grandma gives me candy, I crunch and crunch until it is all gone because it tastes so good! One time Grandma and I had a contest to see who could make their candy last the longest. Grandma won!

I love going on walks with Grandma in her back yard. There is so much to see and do! Grandma's yard is full of flowers, trees, birds, and lots of green grass to run and play on. I like the way the grass tickles my feet when I take my shoes off. I like the way it smells after dad cuts Grandma's grass on a hot summer's day.

There are butterflies of many colors in Grandma's garden. There are a lot of bees too! One time when I was picking a flower for Grandma in her garden, a honey bee stung my finger! Grandma put medicine on the bee sting. The medicine took the pain away.

"Bees are very special," Grandma told me. "They help all our flowers, fruits, and vegetables grow. Without them we would not have food!"

I believe Grandma, but I STILL do not like bee stings.

My favorite memory of Grandma is the time she taught me how to listen to birds. Did you know baby birds learn to sing from their parents? Did you know each bird has a special song? My favorite bird is the red bird.

"The red bird is called a Cardinal," Grandma told me. "Listen to its song."

Now when I hear a sharp, soft *"tweet, tweet, tweet"* sound, I know a cardinal is near. I see red birds all the time now because I know their song. Every time I hear or see one, I think of my Grandma.

I went to see Grandma today. She wanted to walk in the garden. As we walked, I put my hand in Grandma's and squeezed her hand very hard. She squeezed my hand back and that made me feel good.

Grandma was happy. Her eyes twinkled and we laughed and giggled out loud as we walked together. Grandma reached into her pocket and pulled out two pieces of butterscotch candy. One for her and one for me. We crunched and crunched together and had a contest to see who could crunch the loudest. Grandma won!

I felt wonderful walking in Grandma's garden.

"This is a touch-me-not flower," Grandma told me. She showed me the orange flower with tiny green leaves. When Grandma touched the leaves, they folded up! I touched the leaves and they folded up again! Seeing the little leaves fold up made me laugh even more. Grandma was laughing too.

Then something strange happened.

"Oh Johnny, isn't that the funniest thing you ever saw"? Grandma said.

The strange thing is, my name is Mathew. Johnny is my Dad's name. I was not sure what to do.

Then I remembered what Mom and Dad told me. There are times Grandma is confused. When Grandma called me Johnny it did not bother me. She thought I was my Dad. She was smiling and happy!

I felt happy to see her happy.

After we walked in the garden we played a game of hunting for pictures in the clouds. Grandma gave me a big hug. "I love my Johnny boy," she said.

"I love you too," I said.

I was glad to feel her arms around me.

There are days when I visit Grandma she does not feel well. We do not go on walks in her back yard. We do not listen to birds or talk about bees. We do not have butterscotch. Some days she sits in a chair and looks out the window. It makes me feel very sad when Grandma does not want to walk with me in her garden.

"Grandma is going through some changes," Mom told me.

"She will have trouble remembering important things," Dad said.

Sometimes, Grandma has trouble remembering where she is and she gets upset, even mad. I feel sad when Grandma is sad. I wish I could make her happy.

Mom told me that there is a big word adults use for the changes happening to Grandma. It is called *Alzheimer's disease*. Wow, that is a big word! I can't catch Alzheimer's from Grandma, like I can catch a cold.

"Not all people who get older get Alzheimer's," Dad told me.

"It is like when you have a broken arm," Mom said. "Your arm does not move or work the way it is supposed to because it is broken. With Alzheimer's disease, the part of the body that is broken is the brain."

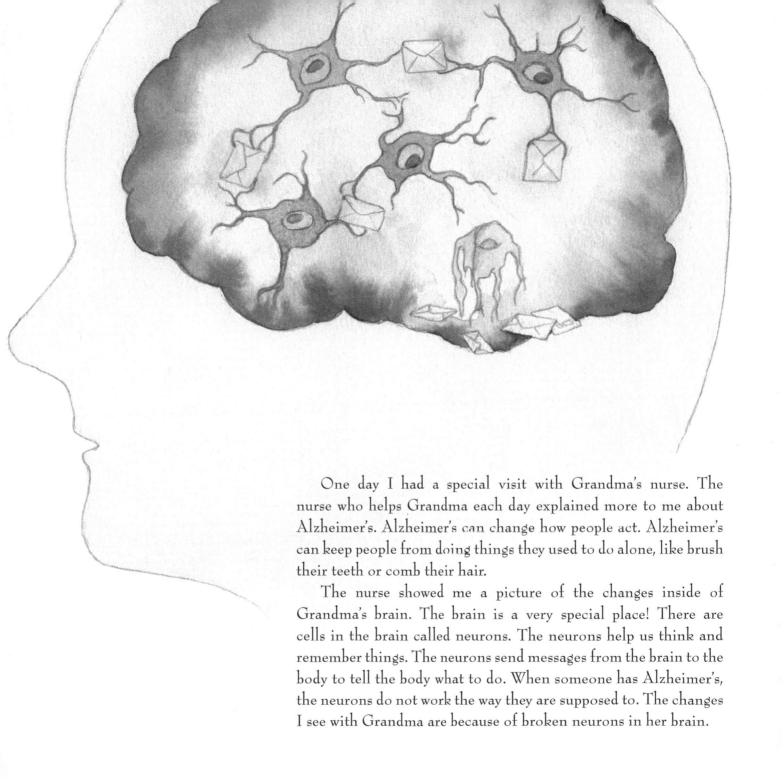

One day I had a special visit with Grandma's nurse. The nurse who helps Grandma each day explained more to me about Alzheimer's. Alzheimer's can change how people act. Alzheimer's can keep people from doing things they used to do alone, like brush their teeth or comb their hair.

The nurse showed me a picture of the changes inside of Grandma's brain. The brain is a very special place! There are cells in the brain called neurons. The neurons help us think and remember things. The neurons send messages from the brain to the body to tell the body what to do. When someone has Alzheimer's, the neurons do not work the way they are supposed to. The changes I see with Grandma are because of broken neurons in her brain.

Grandma can still remember what happened a long time ago but she has trouble remembering what just happened. That's why people with Alzheimer's sometimes call people by other names. Like Grandma does with me. Mom says I look like my Dad did long ago when he was little. My Grandma remembers Dad better from when he was a little boy. For Grandma, it is like she is with him from long ago when she is with me.

It makes me happy to know I can help Grandma by letting her call me by my Dad's name when we spend time together.

Sometimes I miss the way things used to be with Grandma. We did lots of fun stuff together. I used to spend the night at Grandma's house. We watched movies. We made cookies and stayed up late eating them. We counted the stars and told stories until we fell asleep. Grandma told me stories about when she was my age or when Dad was little. I miss spending the night with Grandma.

Now we go to Grandma's house every day to check on her instead of spending the night. We bring her food and make sure the nurse is doing everything Grandma needs.

Some things stayed the same. Grandma and I still like to tell each other stories. I help her remember the parts she forgets. She likes to hear stories about when she was growing up and when my Dad was little.

These are the stories Grandma once told me. Mom said the best stories for Grandma are ones that happened a long time ago. I still remember them, so now I tell her.

They make her smile. Grandma still loves to look out the window and count the stars at night, just like we used to. We still like to eat cookies!

One day when I visited Grandma she was sad. She cried. I don't like it when she cries.

I wanted to help her feel better so I sang our favorite song, *You are my Sunshine*. Grandma smiled and sang with me.

"I can't believe it," Mom said. "Look at how happy she is!"

The nurse said I gave Grandma something called *music therapy*. People with Alzheimer's like Grandma need a lot of therapy. They need to listen to the kind of music they liked when they were very young. They need to be able to do art, make things, and do all kinds of fun activities. The nurse said this is *therapy* for my Grandma.

The next time I visited Grandma I brought crayons and papers. We colored, sang, and even took a walk in her back yard.

I asked Grandma, "Do you want to walk in the garden or sing a song?" I did not ask Grandma, "What do you want to do today?"

Grandma's nurse said the best way for me to talk with Grandma is to use short sentences and to give her easy choices. Having too many choices makes Grandma upset.

Grandma understands me better when I talk with her this way.

I know that some days Grandma does not feel well enough to do things with me. She shows this feeling by how she acts. Sometimes she is sad or upset. When she does feel like doing things with me, we have a lot of fun.

Mom, Dad, the nurse, and even Grandma, all say she feels better when I am with her! The nurse gave me a title of *Special Therapy Assistant* for all the things I do when I visit Grandma. To me it's just me and Grandma being Grandma and me!

There are still a few things about Alzheimer's disease I don't understand. I don't understand why Grandma says its December when it is really July. I don't understand why it makes her upset to tell her she is wrong.

"It's like being on a long journey, Mathew," Mom said. "We are meeting Grandma where she is on her journey."

To me it is like my imagination. When I imagine to be a pirate or a king or a chef. Just like my imagination feels real to me, Grandma's thoughts are real to her.

I do not correct or change what Grandma says, even if it is wrong. Correcting her would make her feel sad. If she says the month is December, and it is really July, I use my imagination and pretend it is December.

"When you imagine with Grandma, you are doing *Meet Me Where I Am Care*," Mom told me.

That is what Grandma needs.

There will be a time in the future when Grandma will need more help. She may need help with getting dressed and eating her food. She may stay in bed a lot. Grandma may say or do things that she usually does not say or do. She may even seem like she is mad or upset with Mom, Dad, or even me. It is not Grandma's fault, or ours.

I know the changes are there because of Alzheimer's and not because of me. Grandma still loves me and I still love her, no matter what changes she goes through.

When Grandma can no longer tell me stories, I will tell her the same stories she always told me. I will let her hold the pictures while I tell the stories because I know that will make her happy.

When Grandma isn't able to talk to me anymore, I will hold her hand and talk to her like I do now. I know she will hear me.

Most of all, though Alzheimer's disease may change Grandma, it will not change me. Grandma and I together will always be Grandma and Me.

A Comprehensive Note to Parents and Caregivers

According to the Alzheimer's Association, every 66 seconds someone in the United States develops Alzheimer's disease (AD). By mid-century someone in the United States will develop the disease every 33 seconds. The journey can be difficult and challenging. However, the journey can also be filled with times of warm interaction, happiness, and connection. Even when the abilities of individuals with dementia begin to fade, the connection between individuals remain. Storybooks are an amazing way to answer a young child's questions while opening the lines of communication between the parent and child. Below are a few additional guidelines to help you navigate the journey with your young child:

Understand the progression of the disease.

No two individuals on the journey with dementia are identical. However, there are similarities. Understanding the similarities and the progression of the disease will help you, the parent, to answer questions as they arise. Dementia is not a specific disease. It is the umbrella term used to describe a wide range of symptoms associated with declines in memory, changes in behavior, and decline in ability that interferes with daily life. Alzheimer's disease is one type of dementia. It is the most common form of dementia and accounts for 60 to 80 percent of all types of dementia. The second most common form of dementia is Vascular Dementia and occurs after a stroke. Diligent researchers are working on a cure, but to date there is no cure.

Alzheimer's disease is progressive and advances slowly through three general stages. In the **early** (mild) stage of AD a person may still function independently (live on their own and drive a car), but they may have difficulty recalling the name of a person they just met, misplace items, and demonstrate difficulty with planning. In the **middle** (moderate) stage of AD a person will require more assistance. They may forget important events including birthdays, not know the day of the week, show difficulty dressing appropriately for the season, and show an increased risk for getting lost. During this stage changes in behavior and personality may occur. Withdrawal, sadness, agitation, irritation, and episodes of paranoia and delusions may occur. In the **late** (severe) stage of AD the person may need constant care. They may need help with dressing, bathing, feeding and be at higher risk for falls/infections/illness that require trips to the emergency department (ED) or hospital. These trips to the ED or hospital can provide challenges for the whole family.

Answer questions in an age appropriate manner.

This book was written to help prepare a young child for the journey with a family member who has AD. No two children are exactly alike. Therefore, the amount of questions you may get from one child can be very different than the amount of questions you receive from another child. Also, some of the questions a child may ask depends on the closeness of the relationship between the child and the adult with the illness. If the child and the adult have a special bond they will likely wonder if they will continue to have a special bond. It is important to reassure young children that their special bond will remain, despite the changes in their interactions.

Whether your child askes a lot of questions or no questions, there are some common things young children wonder about. It is important to express the following to young children: They cannot catch Alzheimer's from their family member. Only some people who get older will develop the illness. Confirm to children that they are not the cause of the changes that occur. The disease is the cause of the changes. Although the disease may change their family member's memory, how they act and what they can do, the love that family member has for the child does not go away.

Reassure children that their feelings are normal.

Just like adults, children experience a wide range of emotions including sadness, anger, fear, guilt and even a sense of loss when dealing with the serious illness of a close family member. Being honest with your feelings as an adult helps reassure your child that his/her feelings are important and normal.

Reassure children that they are not the cause of behavior and personality changes.

Behavioral and personality changes including withdrawal, sadness, agitation, irritation, and episodes of paranoia and delusions may occur. These changes can be distressing for both the adults and children, especially when the behaviors are directed at the family members. It is especially important to remind your child that they are not to blame for the behaviors. The disease is to blame. There are times when these behaviors occur with little warning. During these times gently remove your child from the situation until things are calm again. Never force an interaction between family members.

Allow your child to be part of the family care team.

Young children should never become the caretakers for their grandparents or great-grandparents. This is more likely to occur when a grandparent or great grandparent lives in the same home as the young child. However, there are daily opportunities for your young child to be a helpful member of the family. For instance, getting a glass of water for Grandma, when needed. If there is a change in your child's normal pattern of being––changes in sleep, appetite, mood or behavior––that may be a signal to you that they are taking on more than they can handle at their age.

Young children have a unique ability to bring happiness, fun and energy to a situation. This happy energy can be therapeutic for all family members. Look for opportunities for your child to sing, color, spend time with your loved one. As the disease advances, those opportunities will change, but opportunities for interaction continue.

In this book, we introduce the "meet me where I am" principle. Too often we try to bring people with Alzheimer's into our reality rather than joining them in theirs. The many changes in your family member's brain may prevent him or her from recognizing the current situation and reality. Because of this a grandchild may look like a son, for example. Correcting and trying to force the person with Alzheimer's to "remember" accurately only leads to frustration, sadness and disconnection. When you meet your loved one in his or her reality, your loved one may join you back in yours at another time.

About the Authors

Beatrice Tauber Prior, Psy.D. is a Clinical Psychologist, author, and mother of two young children. Dr. Prior specializes in child development and neuropsychology and has had the privilege of working with many individuals and families over the span of her 25-year career. Inspired by her own children's boundless energy and ability to connect with others, she partnered to write a book that will capture the interest of kids of all ages.

Mary Ann Drummond is a Registered Nurse, dementia educator, and author of *Meet Me Where I Am: An Alzheimer's Care Guide*. Ms. Drummond has a passion for presenting innovative and successful strategies in both caregiver and provider settings to assist individuals with dementia to "live their best" each day. With over thirty years of nursing experience and sixteen years as a VP in the assisted living industry developing programs for dementia care, she credits much of her expert knowledge to the greatest teachers of all, those who live daily with Alzheimer's disease and related dementias. Ms. Drummond enjoys working with organizations across the country to increase successful outcomes in dementia care.